Monroe Community School
Paideia Project
St. Paul, Minnesota

THE MAN
WHO COULD
CALL DOWN OWLS

EVE BUNTING

THE MAN
WHO COULD
CALL DOWN OWLS

ILLUSTRATED BY

CHARLES MIKOLAYCAK

ALADDIN BOOKS
MACMILLAN PUBLISHING COMPANY
NEW YORK

MAXWELL MACMILLAN CANADA
TORONTO

MAXWELL MACMILLAN INTERNATIONAL
NEW YORK   OXFORD   SINGAPORE   SYDNEY

First Aladdin Books edition 1994
Text copyright © 1984 by Eve Bunting
Illustrations copyright © 1984 by Charles Mikolaycak

Aladdin Books
Macmillan Publishing Company
866 Third Avenue
New York, NY 10022

Maxwell Macmillan Canada, Inc.
1200 Eglinton Avenue East
Suite 200
Don Mills, Ontario M3C 3N1

Macmillan Publishing Company is part of the Maxwell
Communication Group of Companies.

Printed in the United States of America

10   9   8   7   6   5   4   3   2   1

Library of Congress Cataloging-in-Publication Data

Bunting, Eve, date.
The man who could call down owls / Eve Bunting ; illustrated
by Charles Mikolaycak. — 1st Aladdin Books ed.
p.   cm.
Summary: When a stranger takes away the powers of an old
man who has befriended owls, the vengeance wreaked on him
is swift and fitting.
ISBN 0-689-71837-3
[1. Owls — Fiction.]   I. Mikolaycak, Charles, ill.   II. Title.
PZ7.B91527Man 1994
[E] — dc20   93-23706

For Candy Dean, who told me
about the man who could call down owls

—E.B.

To Sido Farina

—C.M.

There was once a man who could call down owls. He wore a cloak of softest white and a wide hat with a feather in it, and he carried a willow wand.

Every night, when the dark came, the owl man walked into the woods and stopped at the first clearing. Every night, a scattering of people from the village followed to watch. The boy Con, who lived in the village too, always came.

The owl man stared into the trees. He had shadows on his face but not in his eyes and he made no sound.

The watchers, too, stayed quiet and at a distance.

The owl man stretched his willow wand to the night sky.

And the owls came.
They came swooping on noiseless wings.
To perch on his shoulders.
To perch on his wand.
To gather on branches closest to where he stood.
Always, the owls came.

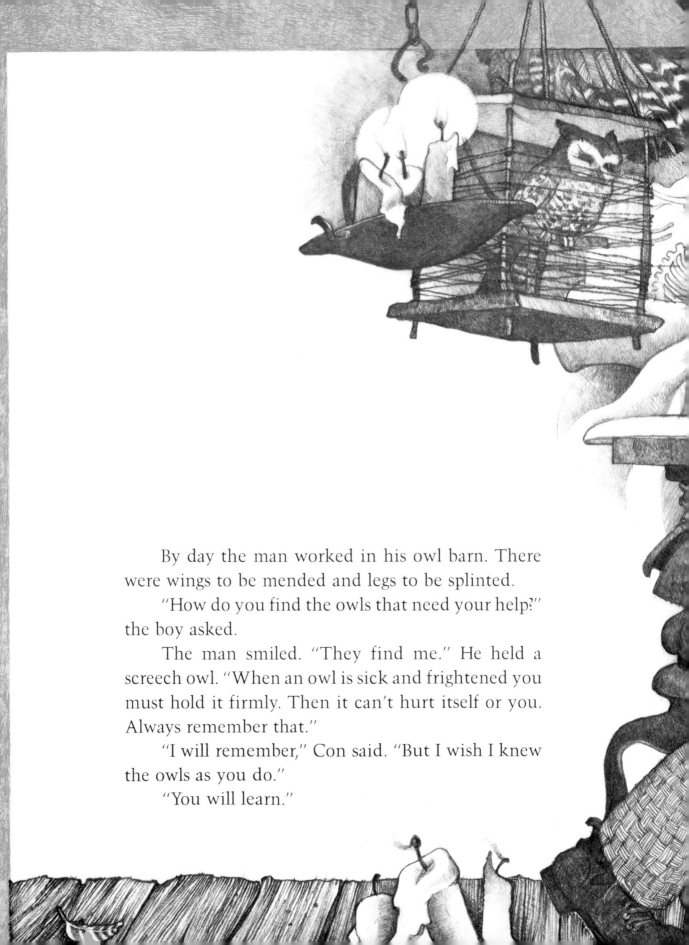

By day the man worked in his owl barn. There were wings to be mended and legs to be splinted.

"How do you find the owls that need your help?" the boy asked.

The man smiled. "They find me." He held a screech owl. "When an owl is sick and frightened you must hold it firmly. Then it can't hurt itself or you. Always remember that."

"I will remember," Con said. "But I wish I knew the owls as you do."

"You will learn."

And now, in the night clearing, the boy moved to the man's side, quietly as an owl in flight.

"What kind is that?" he whispered.

"Barn owl." The man's voice was high and for a minute Con thought the sound of it was the sound of wind in the trees.

The barn owl swiveled its white, flower face, raised its wings, then closed itself again.

An owl no bigger than a sparrow came to nestle in the shadow of the wide hat.

"Elf owl." The man smoothed the pale chest feathers till the owl eyes closed.

Deep in the dark of the trees was a hoot, hoot, hooting and a great horned cut the air to land on a stunted branch, so close that the boy could see the ring of white feathers that lay mysteriously at its throat.

Owls everywhere. And the man in the middle, his cloak drifting about him like marsh mist, and Con, always Con, and the man with the owls around him.

One night a stranger came. His eyes narrowed when the owls dropped from the trees. He stepped close.

"A man who can command the birds of the air has power indeed!" he whispered.

"He does not command," Con said. But the stranger was not listening.

At the next dusk, the man who could call down owls did not walk on the path that led to the woods. The stranger walked. He wore the white cloak and the broad-brimmed hat and in his hand was the willow wand.

Con ran to tug at his cloak. "Where is the man who can call down owls? What have you done with him?"

The stranger pushed the boy aside.

"You took his cloak and his hat and his willow wand," Con said.

"He gave them to me."

"He would never give them."

The stranger smiled. "I took them, then, and his power along with them."

The stranger's smile was cold as death and Con was afraid.

The people clustered behind as the stranger entered the clearing. And it was then that Con saw the great snowy owl. He caught his breath. Never had he seen such a rare and beautiful owl. It shimmered above the clearing, its giant wings whitening the earth below. And Con knew how the stranger came by the cloak and the hat and the willow wand. And he knew that the owl was the man and the man the owl, and that the man who could call down owls would never return.

The stranger raised the wand to point to the moon.

And the owls came.

Con had never seen so many. The sky moved with them.

A hawk owl dropped on pointed wings to hover over the stranger's head, then dived, its talons raking the hat and the hands that the stranger raised to protect himself.

A great gray came, its flight slow and measured. It came silently, on straightened legs, and its beak found the stranger's cheek, and there were other owls, swooping, shearing, searing. The air hissed to the beat

of wings and the stranger was crawling for the shelter
of the trees, running now, the white cloak falling from
him to lie in a drift of snow.

He was gone, and so were the owls. And the people stood, mute, frightened.

Above, the great snowy melted upward to fade into the clouds that covered the moon, drifted up and was gone too.

Then the owls came, swooping on noiseless wings.

To perch on the boy's shoulders.

To perch on his head.

To gather on branches closest to where he stood.

Chirping and screeching and filling the night with love, the owls came.

This book was set in 14-point Trump.
The text was composed by Cardinal Typographers.
Printing done by The Eusey Press.

Typography and binding design by
Charles Mikolaycak and Ellen Weiss.

The drawings were rendered actual size
in pencil on a natural vellum paper
manufactured by Canson & Montgolier Mills
in France.